CITA'S WORLD

Cita

with

Glenda Howard

sepia

BOOKS

BET Publications, LLC
www.bet.com

SEPIA BOOKS are published by

BET Publications, LLC
c/o BET BOOKS
One BET Plaza
1900 W Place NE
Washington, DC 20018-1211

All Kensington Titles, Imprints, and Distributed Lines are available at special quantity discounts for bulk purchases for sales promotions, premiums, fund-raising, and educational or institutional use. Special book excerpts or customized printings can also be created to fit specific needs. For details, write or phone the office of the Kensington special sales manager: Kensington Publishing Corp., 850 Third Avenue, New York, NY 10022, attn: Special Sales Department, Phone: 1-800-221-2647.

ISBN: 1-58314-278-9

First Printing: November 2001
10   9   8   7   6   5   4   3   2   1

Printed in the United States of America

This book is dedicated

to my family, who has instilled in me

the will to succeed.

Acknowledgments

Cita wishes to thank the following people for their love and support: Thanks to my producer, Tracye Kinzer, for holding the team together and keeping me on top of my game; special thanks to Associate Producer Cliff McBean, otherwise known as "Cliff Mack," for the slamming one-liners and for writing scripts that keep it real; big shout-out to Jelani Johnson, the production assistant who keeps everything wrapped up tight; to John Fenton, who keeps me looking fabulous with his virtual magic; much love to my girl, Kittie, who brings yours truly, Ms. Cita, to life every week; big shout-out to Stephen Hill, the big cheese who keeps the BET music division miles ahead of the competition; and thanks to his assistant, Dania Jolley, who knows how to keep everybody in check. Thanks to the rest of the BET staff and the fans—I feel the love!

Glenda Howard wishes to thank the following people: First and foremost, I'd like to thank God for blessing me on this path; special thanks to Linda Gill, publisher of BET books, for bringing me over to the team and giving me this opportunity; big thanks to the *Cita's World* team: Tracye Kinzer, Cliff McBean (aka "Cliff Mack"), Jelani Johnson, John Fenton, and Kittie—you all are a truly talented team who have created magic with *Cita's World;* special thanks to my mother, Mary, and Aunt Josie, who instilled in me the will to succeed; thanks to my husband, Evan King, for his love, support, patience, and understanding; to my sisters, Janice Poole, "the buffest chick at Hollywood Health Club," and Machelle Poole—you both are the best; to my friends Deggra Stratton and Cheryl Mitchell—remember the good times we had at QPTV?; and special thanks to those folks who inspired me along the way.

Table of Contents

Introduction

What's up, everybody?

I hope all of you are doing well. Well, those rumors you heard were true. Cita has written a book. I was constantly being asked questions from the fans and the media about my personal life. Everyone wanted to know what kind of men I have dated, would I really date a man who wasn't a baller, what my opinion is about certain celebrities, and which artists need to sit down. Everybody wants to know about Ms. Cita. Ever since my show relocated to New York City, I have become an instant celebrity. I just want y'all to know that I am very grateful that *Cita's World* has blown up, and that I am now a household name. My life has gotten hectic, but I wouldn't change a thing, and I still love you all.

This book is dedicated to my fans and will give a little peek inside my world. In the past I have caught a lot of static from folks who got mad when I gave my opinion about certain things. Hey, I'm sorry if the truth hurts, but the one thing I do is keep it real. So if you can't stand the heat, you need to get the hell out of the kitchen. That's right, hold me down, I'm getting started.

Now, y'all know I'd love to hear from you, so when you get a chance, drop me a line at: *Cita's*

World, 105 East 106th Street, New York, NY 10029, or hit me off with an E-mail at www.BET.com/Cita.

Until then, take care.
Buh bye,
Cita

Media Hype

The Jerry Springer Show

Mamacita wants to know: How does Jerry Springer continually get the biggest fools in America on his show? Do they post notices on every telephone pole in the trailer parks and projects advertising a free hot meal and two dollars to appear on the show? And why does everybody appear so damned shocked when they find out their boyfriend/girlfriend/husband/wife/transvestite gay lover is cheating on them? First of all, when you get a phone call to see Jerry, you know they are setting yo butt up.

Let me break it down for you: If your man is out every night until six in the morning and he doesn't work the night shift, he's cheating on you. Or, if the same number keeps showing up on his beeper and he gives you a dumb-ass look claiming he doesn't know who it is,

2

but wants to call them back every time, he is cheating on you. But if you choose to believe the fairy tales, then you deserve to get caught out there on the *Jerry Springer Show*.

If a jigga is doing me wrong, I don't have to get on Jerry's show to set things straight. I'll have the crowd yelling *Cita! Cita! Cita!* as I open up a can of ass whooping and handle my business.

Friends Television Show

Cita wants to holla at ya about the *Friends* show. Where do those giddy white folks get off without having any black friends, neighbors, or coworkers? I mean, can a sista or brother get some love? Everybody on that show is lily-white and happy with big Kool-Aid grins. They are living phat in big-ass, fancy apartments far away from the projects and section-eight housing. I guess they feel they're going to have to beef up security if they change the color scheme. Listen up, NBC, before I scream on you! Get real and put some flava up in the mix. At least put a Puerto Rican on the *Friends* show, and don't call the only one in town who's working: J.Lo with the big butt. Or go to East LA and hire a Mexican to play a postal worker. Jesse Jackson, where are you? We need you to get the Rainbow Coalition over there and shake things up—keep hope alive.

4

UPN

Okay, I watch UPN because they try and represent. But why do the commercials advertising their shows make everybody look so happy, like they're so relieved to have a steady job? Word. Everybody is smiling so hard like they just got paid and have just enough money to keep the landlords and bill collectors off their backs for one more month. Now don't start blowing up my phone, getting mad at me, telling me, "Cita, you ain't right." I'm keeping it real.

Let Cita put this in yo ear. I will give UPN props for having black shows on their lineup, but do they all have to be shown on the same night? It's like Monday night from eight to ten is prime time for the black shows. Can't they schedule more of them throughout the week? It's like miss Monday and that's it. So don't pick that night to do anything if you want to see your shows; I

know I'm not. Listen to Cita and heed my warning—
don't do your laundry, get yo braids done, hang out with
your homeboy or homegirl, visit your mother, father,
grandmother, or baby's mama on that night, 'cause once
you miss it, you've got to wait a whole 'nother seven
days to catch black night again.

Girlfriends

Ms. Cita's got some real issues with the show *Girlfriends.* Y'all know the show where Diana Ross's daughter plays Joan the lawyer. Okay, reality check one-two, one-two. Joan has a dizzy, chickenhead roommate who doesn't work, eats up all the food in the fridge, and goes in her closet and wears all her designer clothes. Helllllo, if you wear my clothes, dirty them up with yo funk, and won't take them to the dry cleaners 'cause you claim you're broke, those are fighting words. You ain't no friend of mine, more like public enemy number one. Don't get me wrong, I don't condone violence, but I will pull my earrings off, put vaseline on my face, and open up a serious can of ass whooping. Ms. Cita don't play that mess.

The other friend is a gold digger who's always looking for a baller. She borrows money from Joan and never pays her back. Whenever she's got extra money, she'll claim she has to make a car payment or get a new pair of Prada shoes. That heifer has a problem with her priorities. Cita would cut her ass off in a minute.

The last friend is the ghetto-fabulous secretary who's always coming into work fifteen minutes late, talking that same old yada dada about the bus was late. Then she's got the nerve to try and tack on extra minutes to her lunch break. These are not friends, these are trifling chickenheads taking advantage of Joan's kindness. Wake up and smell the coffee, girlfriend!

Judge Mathis

Judge Mathis is the only judge in the system representing the hood, he's strictly from the streets. When he comes into the courtroom, he walks with a swagger, and he sits behind the bench posing in a gangsta lean. The jury is chanting, "Here comes da judge. Here comes da judge. Look out, everybody, 'cause here come da judge." A man of the law, Judge Mathis knows how to talk with the brothers, giving shout-outs like, "Yo, Pookie, they got you on lockdown, too? Don't worry, I'ma hook you up." Now don't get Cita wrong about Judge Mathis, he ain't no pushover. When you step to him, you better step correct, otherwise you're gonna see some neck swiveling and serious attitude from him when he hands down a sentence on yo ass.

But that's my boo. He is the only judge who can

dress *GQ* fly, always glossin' and flossin'. Check out the ice on his hands, bling-bling! Judge Mathis can keep it real, but on the down low, hush-hush, and the Q-Tip, I think he's hiding a forty-ounce under them robes, but re-member you didn't hear that from me.

ER

Let me holla at ya! Is there a doctor in the house? Dr. Benton is the only black surgeon operating in the ER. He's holding it down every week. Cita needs a baller like Dr. Benton to keep her flossin' in designer gear. Now I usually don't date a man like Dr. Benton who's so intense. Loosen up, boo-boo, it's not like you just killed somebody. Damn, but in your case you could have. Anyhoo, that fine honey needs a good woman. They hooked him up that trampy chick from the Ally McBeal show, you know, the one with the hair that looks like it was cut with a hatchet. She is in serious need of a beautician's touch—or maybe a magician's. That's right, I said it, I'm not hating up in here, just stating the facts. Dr. Benton, you need a strong, fine, sexy woman such as myself, not no whining chickenhead. Come on over here, baby. I must confess, a little Cita magic can take care of yo stress. Hold me down, big boy!

11

Sex and the City

What is the fascination with that show? Four skinny white chicks hanging out in bars, smoking, drinking martinis and cosmopolitans, talking about men they want to get with. That show is so unrealistic. How do those chickenheads get a date with a different man every weekend? They don't look that good, and they're all so damn bony. If they were packing more junk in the trunk, I could see why men would be all up in their faces.

Personally speaking, Ms. Cita is a gorgeous, superfine woman, but even I stay home sometimes to get rest. You can't parade through the streets every night in four-inch heels—yo damn feet will start hurting after a while. Somebody hold me down, but I just got to give a comment about wild-ass Samantha, the biggest hoochie to ever hit television. Her track record of getting with so many men is exhausting. She should charge by the hour, make some extra money for herself. Samantha is so damn loose she can't even remember who she brought home last month. She'll chase after any man who's within grabbing distance. Shoot, all those girls must run their own 1-900 number advertising hot free love for all the action they get. Somebody holla at me and give me a clue, I'm confused.

Who Wants to Be a Millionaire

I tried out for the show and got to meet Regis. He told me in order to win a million dollars I had three life-lines and couldn't miss any of the questions. Three life-lines and all those hard-ass questions he was asking me? I started hollering, "Oh, come on, Regis, you need to hook a sista up. Give me a few more lifelines." Well, needless to say, he didn't listen to me. I got down to the last lifeline and called my girl, LaKeisha. Now why did I pick that blabbermouth? Regis told her she only had thirty seconds to answer the question. That fool burned up the time giving shout-outs to everybody she knew. I swear when Regis told me I lost I wanted to raise up and smack that smug look off his face. I started screaming for another chance. It got ugly when security dragged me from the chair. The situation got worse when I called him a midget in a suit. He turned so red I thought he would have a stroke. Oh, well, I guess Ms. Cita needs to stick with the lotto as a get-rich scheme.

Chains of Love

One of the producers for *Chains of Love* called me up and asked if I wanted to be on the show. That fool said he heard I was between dates and being a participant would help me to find a man. First of all, excuse you, I didn't know my business was all up in the streets like that. Damn, people are sweating me, clocking all my moves. I started going off on him. Cita ain't no charity case, I can find me a baller when I need to. Then he started apologizing, begging me to consider, saying it would be a lot of fun and my presence would help boost the ratings. I'm sorry, but being part of a chain gang is not my idea of having a good time. Let me get this straight, Cita is supposed to get chained to three men, who all may be ugly as hell. Hey, if I could choose a man to get chained to I'd pick somebody fine, not some man whose bad breath is going to knock me out or who's going to pass gas and then look at me all funny like it was me. Let me come at you one mo time, I'm not and will never be that hard up to get a date. I am just too damn fine, aiiright. Anyhow, I told those producers that show would never work. Once again, Cita was right.

Judge Judy

Will somebody holla at Cita and please tell me why I would ever go and see Judge Judy if I had a problem? I swear, she is the meanest, crankiest, most evil judge I've ever seen. She looks like she should be sucking on a lemon while flying around the courtroom on a broom. Straight up, she snaps your head off before you can even get the words out your mouth. Innocent or not, Judge Judy treats everybody like they're on the FBI's most wanted list and she's the one who's going to personally hit the switch for the electric chair. They should at least put a sign outside her courtroom warning everybody that they are about to enter the chamber of doom. ENTER AT YOUR OWN RISK.

Josie and the Pussycats

Somebody offered me free tickets to see the *Josie and the Pussycats* movie. I looked at them like they was crazy. One night I was watching television and caught a commercial advertising the movie. Damn, I reached for my remote control real quick to lower the volume. Their singing sounded like a bunch of screeching cats getting dipped in hot water. Personally, I would have to be drunk and two seconds from passing out just to get through the opening credits. Apparently I wasn't the only one who felt this way, because the movie bombed on day one. Doesn't anybody know what a good music sound-track is anymore? Big hint—familarize yo'self with the theme from *Shaft*. Can you dig it?

The WWF

Oh, my Gawwwwd. . . . Cita just loves the men of the World Wrestling Federation, especially The Rock. Tall, muscular, handsome men with lots of duckets to keep Ms. Cita bling-blinging. I went to Madison Square Garden to see *WWF Smackdown* and had a front-row seat. Shoot, you know with me it's first class all the way. Don't even be trying to put me in them seats way up in the nosebleed section. If my man bought those second-class tickets, I would break up with his ass on the spot. I will go off on a jigga, it don't matter where we at. And if he tries to shush me while I'm doing it, Cita gonna start talking louder. Anyhoo, I was solo that night, and The Rock looked at me and my fine self and gave me the eyebrow look, y'all know what I'm talking about. I screamed out, "Rock, let me holla at ya." Just then Chyna, that huge, steriod-injected woman with bulging muscles, came up and got in my face, blocking my action with The Rock. Chyna is a major playa hater, and if it wasn't for Stone Cold Steve Austin pulling me off her, I would have given her a beatdown with my Gucci pumps. I would have hated to ruin a good pair of shoes, but sometimes you've got to teach folks a lesson that they obviously didn't learn at home.

Cita's Thoughts on Reality Television

Television is really getting out of hand. What are those television executives doing in the boardroom, sitting around the conference room table sniffing glue and passing around crack pipes, coming up with wild ass shows like *Survivor* and *Boot Camp?* Cita's going to drop some knowledge right about now. Black people usually don't apply for crazy-ass shows like this. First of all, when they invented bungee jumping, you ain't never seen no black folks participate in a game where they tie a rope around their ankles and throw themselves off a bridge. You have to be crazy as hell to do something like that. Yeah, I know the prize money of a million dollars for being the champion on *Survivor* will make a brother or sister take a pause for the cause. They'll start thinking about getting a brand new Beemer or a shiny phat Benz, but when they think about the torture they have to go through, reality sets in and they'll ask themselves, "Have I lost my damn mind?" To further make my point, let's discuss them show by show.

Survivor

Let me break it down. First of all, a fine sista like myself does not like to sleep on a mud-caked floor with a bunch of strange-ass folks under a tent. They don't provide you with a blanket, pillows, or a damn bed. Those producers are crazy! Second of all, I need quiet. Cita will smack somebody upside their head if they don't shut up with all the yacking so I can get some sleep. Third, I can't survive two months in the wilderness without getting my hair did! A sista needs a touch-up to keep her hair fly. I refuse to look busted on national television—too many jiggas who want to get with me will be watching. Fourth, my nails. I have to get my acrylic tips filled, painted, and airbrushed every two weeks like clockwork. Shoot, I'll race the Korean owner to the shop just to be the first in line. Fifth, I like to sleep late. Don't be getting me up at the crack of dawn to go and try to catch some fish for breakfast. Let's get real, sistas and brothers want some bacon, eggs, grits, and toast in the morning. Now, I know y'all are going to blow up my phone and say Gervase on Survivor I, and Alicia on Survivor II were holding it down and representing. Okay, let me keep it real up in here. Those two knew they weren't going to win, but they had a plan. Why do you think Gervase was always grinning at the camera? He was chasing a movie deal. No way in hell could homeboy have been that happy. As for Alicia, she made sure to always dress in skimpy clothes to show off her muscles because she was scheming for an endorsement deal. Anyway, wonder woman could deal with starving because she wanted to keep her stomach tight and flat. As for me, I have a weakness for pork fried rice and chicken wings from the local Chinese takeout. Hunting rats for dinner just does not do it for me. I don't give a damn how much they claim it tastes like chicken, they can kiss my ass. Ms. Cita is not eating any rats.

Boot Camp

Sexy Mamacita does not like loud, rude people in uniform yelling all in her ear. Shoot, it feels like you're in some kind of maximum security correctional facility, or on some serious lockdown. If you want me in the army, you better start a war and bring back the draft. Once Ms. Cita heard about the requirements for *Boot Camp*, I knew it was not for me. First of all, they put you in a camouflage uniform, which is not flattering on every-body. Excuse me, but can I at least wear Fubu or Phat Farm, that is more of my style and taste. Then, they want to cut your hair. Hold up, wait a damn minute. Nobody but Cita's personal hairstylist, Grace from 125th Street in Harlem, is allowed to touch her hair. A lot of these folks are playa haters and they will jack your hair up on pur-pose. Once again, this is another show where they wake you up at five o'clock in the morning. I'll say it again, Cita is not a morning person. Can they at least hook a sister up with a cup of coffee to get her started? Then, they want you to do sit-ups, push-ups, go running for five miles. Oh, hell, I failed physical education in high school. I know this show is not for me. Enough said.

Battle Dome

I was chilling, watching late-night television last week, and caught this show called *Battle Dome*. It's a game show where people pumped up on steroids and built like amazons and gladiators chase you around an obstacle course trying to inflict bodily harm on you. For example, the contestant is supposed to chase a hoop on a string and try and throw a ball through it. That sounds easy except for the fact you've got a seven-foot giant waiting to give you whiplash as you try to score. Then, they've got this segment where you have to jump over a series of hurdles for some lousy points. As you jump over each hurdle, a gladiator is ready to take yo ass out in midair. And once they crack your damn ribs or kneecap, they stand and yell insults as you're lying on the floor in pain. That's whack. I'm from the hood, you don't give me a beatdown on national television and then get up in my face laughing at me. Ain't nothing funny about this situation. Cita will have to tell the ref to punch the stop clock, this game is over. Now it's time to play by my rules. I will get on my cell phone and call my dawgs to come down to the station to play a game called We Gonna Whip Yo Ass Until You Cry for Yo Mama.

Fear Factor

My girlfriend Laquida wanted me to join her as a contestant on the *Fear Factor* show. She had just broken up with this baller named Hi-Time and needed some cash. Laquida is one of those lazy chicks who never worked a day in her life, and she wasn't about to go apply for a real job. So when she heard that the *Fear Factor* show was offering money to the winners, she thought that was her ticket to easy street. We met with the producers of the show who told us what we would have to do as a competitor. There were three tests to pass, and the last man standing gets the prize. The first test was to hold onto a rope attached to a runaway horse and let it drag you for a mile. I wasn't feelin' that scenario too good, especially when I saw that wild-eyed, foaming-at-the-mouth beast that was going to pull you through the streets. That horse had a nasty look on his face and you knew he was going to give you the ride of your life. The second test was to lie down in a pine box that resembled a coffin and have 300 snakes crawl across your body for sixty seconds. All bets were off after I heard that. I started cussing those producers out and told them they were crazy. It was quite obvious to me that whoever was coming up with these ideas had been tripping on drugs and needed some serious rehab. Laquida begged for me to calm down and sign up. I jumped out of my chair and lunged for her and those producers had to hold me back. My hand was aching to slap that silly heifer. I told her to take her trifling ass down to Burger King and get herself a job flipping burgers and cooking fries. Laquida's biggest fear should now be if I'm still mad and want to kick her ass for trying to get me involved in some mess like that.

Temptation Island

Personally, I think this is one of the most craziest ass shows on television. One day my boo, Carlos, told me he signed us up to be a couple on *Temptation Island*. I looked at him like he was out of his mind. He said it would be a terrific way to get a free vacation in paradise. Excuse you, but I don't consider it a good experience when a bunch of money hungry hoochies with fake boobs start grinning all up in my man's face. The purpose of this show is to see if your relationship could last when those scheming hoochies tempt your man with their big asses. Meanwhile, the staff is giggling as they videotape all the action. Then they have the nerve to show you the tape to make sure you know what's going on behind your back. Did y'all catch those episodes where the women are crying after they see their man with another woman? This show is a setup for an ass kicking. I'm going to keep it real. If somebody shows me a videotape of my man all over another woman I'm going to find the nearest coconut tree on that island. Ms. Cita is going to get a couple of coconuts and start practicing her fastball. Let me say this, the madder I am, the more perfect my aim. A couple of people will have some knots upside their head before I leave that hot little island. Believe me, when Cita gets through with them they'll change the name from Temptation Island to the Island of Fear. Believe that.

The Grammy Awards

The Grammy Awards is Cita's time to shine. That's right, hold me down. This is the show where everybody tries to compete with the beautiful one—Cita dearest. I always look good and the designers are blowing up my phone begging me to wear their gear. That's right, I got Versace, Fendi, Prada, Aramani, and Valentino beeping and paging me. All the haters and chickenheads need to sit down, it's Cita's world. Yeah, yeah, I know I'm not a recording artist, but I am the sexiest VJ out there. Jennifer Lopez tried to upstage me one year wearing that green dress, but word, she strictly came in second place next to me. Then bony-roni Toni Braxton tried to grab the spotlight by wearing that dress that looked like a cut up shower curtain with a belt. Listen, honey, desperation can lead to bad decisions. Nobody can compete with the fabulous one. Ladies, next year take Cita's advice and put some clothes on.

Source Awards

The Source Awards is the only show where a bullet-proof vest is a fashion accessory—or should I say, it's a necessity. Yours truly, the ghetto-fabulous goddess of music videos, was hosting the show when a fight broke out backstage and in the balcony. I was so mad when they stopped taping the show. I was wearing a gorgeous green Gucci dress and some slamming Manolo Blahnik shoes and looked damn good. But, despite the inevitable high ratings that my beauty would have brought them, my segment was cut. At this time, I want to call out all the perpetrators who swagger up to the stage to accept their awards and take an hour to thank God over and over again. Then in the next few minutes they have a forty-ounce bottle of malt liquor in one hand, and the other hand is swinging a fist. Next time y'all want to fight, wait until you get back to your crib before you start riffing. Don't blow my opportunity to shine. I've got blinding star power—stop trying to keep Cita down. Thankfully, only the VIPs were allowed in for the follow-up show. The playa haters will never be able to keep a good woman like me down.

BET Awards Show

Did y'all check out the first BET Awards Show? Now, I'm not going to say too much about the folks who hand me my weekly paycheck—Ms. Cita ain't no fool. But, I did want to make a few comments about the show. First of all, somebody needs to tell those artists who attend the show that this is not the place to announce when your album is going to drop, or when your clothing line is going to hit the store. If they want the public to know this information, somebody needs to tell their cheap asses to pay for the advertisement. Second of all, folks need to recognize who's the big cheese at this function—it's me, Cita, baby. BET gave Whitney Houston some kind of special achievement award, which should have gone to me. I'm not playa hating but it's time that folks started passing trophies my way. But, the comment that really irked my nerves was when Whitney said Bobby Brown was the original king of rhythm and blues. I had to restrain myself from snatching the microphone from her and asking if she was out of her mind. Ms. Cita did not take it there because I know Whitney and me would have been throwing down on that stage and Bobby would have tried to jump in and break us up. And it wouldn't be right to get caught fighting on national television.

The Dating Game

The Users

I went out with this jigga who told me I was the finest woman he ever met. I felt he was pretty honest, so I went out on a date with him. But every time we went out he kept asking questions about my job and all the famous celebrities I get to mingle with. He wanted to visit me at the studio and begged for VIP passes to all the events. I found out Tyrone was scheming to get my VJ job with BET when I saw him talking to my executive producer. He was showing his best "Cita" imitation, doing my dance moves and my gestures. I was so mad I took a bottle of Cristal and drenched that fool. Everybody thought I was playa hating, but I had to shut him down before my producers got any brilliant ideas.

Missing-in-Action Wallet

Don't you just hate those cheap men who always try to run a game on you? The number one game is, I'm sorry but I left my wallet at home. I went out with this man to the movies and when we get to the window he claimed he only had enough cash for his ticket. I was highly upset, but I paid for my ticket anyway because I wanted to see the new Denzel Washington movie. Then we get inside and he starts ticking off a list of items he wants me to get at the food counter like Bon Bons, popcorn, soda, M&Ms, and a hot dog. I gave him this evil nasty look and said if I got the food how could he possibly eat it if his teeth were missing? He thought I was joking and said he didn't have any missing teeth. I told him he would if I got the food. All I can say is he lost his appetite real quick.

Liars

Cita has dated her share of lying men. I met this man at a club who told me he was a pilot for a major airline. Every time he saw me he had a souvenir from a foreign country. Boy, I started bragging to everybody that my new boo was all that. I was so impressed that every time I had to book a flight I would use the one he worked for in the hopes that maybe I'd get a glimpse of him in his pilot's uniform. Well, one day while I was at Kennedy Airport I caught him all right. Turns out he was a baggage handler who got to load the suitcases onto the damn plane. Oh yeah, I also found out all those souvenirs came from a local ninety-nine-cent store in Times Square.

Disappearing Acts

I dated this jigga for about a year, but he always managed to start an argument and break up with me around the holidays, and then a few weeks later we would make up. After a while, I would look at the calendar and it would be like, okay, my birthday is in the next few weeks, time for Leon to pull a disappearing act. Finally I decided to get the jump on him. I flipped the script and broke up with him. The next week he had the nerve to knock on my door with a stupid grin on his face. He said look and turned his back to me and pointed to his head. He had my name carved into his hair. He said this proves I really love you. I looked at that fool and his haircut and slammed the door as hard as I could.

Scrubs

A good looking man can make you lose your mind and lower your standards. Aiiright, Cita admits that she dated this fine guy named Tyrese who was a scrub. Tyrese lived in the basement of his momma's house, didn't have a car, and worked construction here and there. He claimed he was low on funds since he was between jobs, so I didn't scream on him when we walked into McDonald's. I won't front and say I wasn't mad to be at a fast-food joint on the first date, Ms. Cita was too through, but I let it go. But after Tyrese ordered our food, he pulled out a pocketful of food stamps to pay for the bill. I was so embarrassed that I started walking backward—right out the door. I haven't heard from Tyrese since that date. Like my girls from TLC said, "No more scrubs for me."

YMCA

Word of advice: Never date a man who you meet outside the YMCA. I don't care how buffed his body is and how much he tries to convince you that he only uses the facility for the gym. Too many guys hanging in front of the YMCA are temporarily homeless and they're looking for a softhearted woman to provide them some free shelter. I'm not admitting if this particular situation has happened to me or not. Cita will only say one thing, love will make you do foolish things.

Old Men

One night I was kinda bored so I went to this bingo party. The place was packed with senior citizens. I met this man named Charles who kept saying we were the only young ones in the place. Charles looked good for his age, but I suspected he was a senior citizen, too. His teeth were perfect, but when he laughed they seemed to shift. And his black hair started looking a little blue—probably from too much hair dye. Finally, I got my answer about his age. I saw him getting on the bus with a senior citizen pass. I yelled out to him and he tried to act like he didn't know me. Since he was cold busted, he told me that I was mistaken, he was Charles' father, that I knew his son. I have to tell you that was a pitiful excuse and I told his old ass about himself.

Good Hair

I met this man who had a head full of waves on top of his head. He told me his mother had Indian blood and that's why he had pretty hair. Well, the next month that pretty hair started resembling a Brillo Pad after too many uses—hard, wiry and bushy. Why can't men just admit they went to the store and bought "Indian blood in a jar," otherwise known as a perm?

Funkmeisters

Watch out for those men who ask you out for a date but don't believe in taking a bath. I was headed to dinner with this jigga who looked fly in his Fubu gear. But once we got in the car, I kept smelling something musty and after a while the smell was overwhelming. I was becoming lightheaded from trying to hold my breath. Shoot, sometimes you just have to get blunt, so I just came out and asked him if he took a bath today. He had the nerve to get indignant at my question, telling me no, but he had on clean clothes. That man had the nerve to say there's nothing as sexy as the smell of the human body. Obviously, he couldn't smell his own funk 'cause there was nothing sexy about it.

Bad Breath

Watch out for those dates with that serious halitosis problem. Is Cita lying when she says that smelling bad breath can kill you? I went out on a blind date with this guy who was gorgeous. But, damn, once he stopped smiling and started talking my eyes started to cross from the fumes coming out of his mouth. He asked me if there was a problem, and I said yes. The first stop for this date is to the drugstore to get your ass some Scope, some toothpaste and a toothbrush, because your funky breath can cause a homicide. I know that was rude, but the truth ain't never killed nobody yet.

Suspect

Cita's got a test if you suspect that the man you're dating is gay. If he admires my clothes then he's got good taste. But if he keeps complimenting, let's say, my shoes, I will try the test on him. I'll take my shoes off and walk out the room, and then I'll sneak back in. If he's trying to put his big foot in my Christian Dior pump, I consider it a sign—he's gay and we won't be taking that big walk down the aisle. Cita and her man cannot wear the same sexy high-heeled pumps. That's a little too freaky and let's end it right there.

Fake Hair

Why can't men be honest about the fake stuff they wear? I went out with this dude who wore his hair in an Afro. That was cool and all, but somehow his hair never looked right to me. The color in the center of his head never matched the other sections. So, y'all know me, I came out and asked him if he wore a piece. He denied that fact so hard, I thought he was going to have a nervous breakdown. Fine. The next date we went to the amusement park (my choice). I picked the fastest roller coaster with the steepest loops and twists for us to ride. That last loop pulled that rug right off his head. My suspicions were confirmed.

Sound Systems

Why do guys invest all their money in the sound system of their cars? Everybody wants to pretend they're a baller. It seems that men have this contest that whoever has the loudest bass, woofers, and tweeters has da bomb car. Some men put so much money into the music system it's more valuable than the car. Cita knows, because I've seen some hooptie doopties that look like they were one step from being used for scrap metal at the junk yard. These cars had huge speakers in the trunk, along with a twelve-CD disc changer. Inside the car they had television screens in the headrests, and a DVD player. But when they would turn on the system, every window would rattle to the point of almost breaking, and the doors would shake off their hinges. Now that's pathetic.

The Beggars

Watch out for those overly romantic men who want to wine and dine you. I went out with this fine man. He was so good looking he could be called pretty. Every time we went out he bought roses for me. When I came home from a hard day he would massage and kiss my feet. Cita thought she had found the one. I was ready to settle down. Then things changed. He would start begging me for money every time I saw him. I got fed up and asked what he did with his money. He said he was saving it for a sex change operation and was hoping I could help pay for it. Damn, you've got to watch out for those real pretty men, they've got all types of tricks in their bag.

Ugly

Sometimes when you feel really desperate you'll let your guard down. Your love life is in a rut so you'll say yes to that blind date. I was in that particular state of mind when my date knocked at the door and I opened it. He was so ugly he scared me—I just knew he was an alien—no human being could be that gruesome. Just then I snapped back to reality and told him I had a headache and couldn't go out with him. Then I closed the door real fast and waited for my heart to stop racing. My friends think I'm crazy, but I'm still listening to the news for confirmation of a UFO sighting. I'm just know he was too ugly to be human.

No Talent

Why is it that people who think they can sing always feel like they should be in front of an audience? I met Lewis and he thought he was born to be the next Luther Vandross. The only problem was his singing made the hair on the back of my neck stand straight up. His voice was so irritating it sounded like nails on a chalkboard. And how come the mama of these no-talents are always encouraging the nonsense? Lewis's mama smiled at me and said, "Can't my baby sing?" I was having a Cita moment and said if I was deaf I'd still be able to tell that he has no singing talent. Lewis and his mama got mad at me. They were planning on asking me to use my connections and get him on *BET Live*. I fell off my chair laughing. It was the best joke I'd heard in a long time.

Mama's Boy

Watch out for those men who want you to pamper them. Especially the ones who always compare you to their mama. Then they'll start asking you to cook for them. Cita's got a trick for their behinds. I started seeing Tyrone, who was nothing but a mama's boy. He asked me to make him dinner, so I cooked fried chicken, rice, collard greens, and some biscuits. Tyrone said the chicken tasted like wood, the rice was so sticky he couldn't swallow it, the greens were so gritty he almost chipped a tooth, and the biscuits were so hard they could be used as weapons. Hey, Cita said she'd cook, but I never said it would be good. From then on, he never asked me to go near the stove again. Guess I'm a take-out type of girl.

Alibi

I dated this guy one time who tried to play me for a serious fool. I drove over to surprise him at his apartment and caught him kissing a woman in front of his building. Boy, was I mad. All I could do was honk the horn to let him know I had caught his butt; then I drove home. Do you know he came to my house an hour later and asked me what was wrong? I hollered at him that I just saw him kissing another woman. He tried to pull Shaggy's song out of the bag. That fool started singing the lines from "It Wasn't Me." I said don't even go there because when I put my size-eight shoe up your ass, I'm going to be the one telling the judge, that wasn't my Prada shoe they found wedged up your butt.

Mistaken Identity

Mamacita went out for a couple of months with this music executive and I was head-over-heels in love. Derrick claimed he always had to travel out of town, but the strange thing is I kept seeing his car parked in front of this hoochie's house. It was hard to miss his car because it was a bright red Benz with a license plate that read HOTLUVER. I kept questioning him, but he always said it was a case of mistaken identity. I was tired of getting played and made up my mind his game was up. The next time I saw his car at the hoochie's house, I went to the store and bought ten bags of ice and five gallons of ice cream. I pried open his sunroof and dumped the loose cubes all over his seats. Then, I scooped out the ice cream and threw it all over the dashboard. I'm quite sure the sight of all that cold liquid cooled Mr. Hot Luver down.

Thug Life

Cita took a walk on the wild side and decided to go out with a man who had the thuggish appeal. This roughneck brother named Terrence stepped to me wearing baggy jeans, tims, and a wicked scar. I said to myself, he's cute, let me get with him for a while. Homeboy showed up at my house at six o'clock one evening with two snarling pit bulls named Smith and Wesson that he said were his protection because people were looking for him. I got nervous, but decided to hang. Since he was on probation and had to be back home at a certain time, we went to his place. Well, a few minutes later the FBI was swarming his place. Terrence pulled a gun and bullets started flying. I was so scared. When they finally arrested Terrence, I had to convince the FBI that I was Cita from BET and was totally innocent.

I promised them an autographed picture and a shout-out on television if they didn't take me in. Well, Cita is now scared straight. No more thug life for me.

The Saint

After the thug life, I met a man in church. Calvin was real nice, but he was always dropping to his knees and screaming out Hallelujah at the most inappropriate times. Okay, I'm a grateful person, too, but he went overboard. We would walk back to the car and notice that the meter expired, but luckily he didn't get a parking ticket. He would drop to his knees and yell Hallelujahs. We would go to the supermarket and his favorite breakfast cereal, Lucky Charms, was on sale. He would start yelling Hallelujahs. Shoot, he was a nice man but it got to be real embarrassing hanging around him so I had to let him go.

Creative Types

Cita is going to give it to you straight. You've got to watch out for those men who don't want to work. Y'all know them, the so-called creative types who claim they need to stay home and write poetry or compose music. They can't work a nine-to-five job like the rest of us because that would be too distracting to their career. But when you get home from your job and ask them to show you what they were working on, they will claim they had writer's block. But somehow they will always find the right words to ask you for the Benjamins you made on your job.

Young Boyz

My girlfriend Tracee told me that sometimes dating a younger man could be more adventurous than dating older men. Tracee and her new man went out motorcycling and biking. Yeah, it's cool that they can play Genesis, PlayStation, and Nintendo together, but he also had posters of Britney Spears, Brandy, and 3LW on the wall. Wait a minute, just how young *is* he? Tracee said he didn't have a high school diploma yet. She got mad when I asked is that because he's under eighteen and didn't graduate from high school yet? Or he's now an old-ass man trying to act young and never got a high school diploma because he was too dumb to get it?

Fashionably Yours

Why do black people love to pour a whole bottle of baby powder on themselves after they take a shower? Do they need to let the whole world know they just finished bathing? Excuse me, but it looks like they've been playing in flour. That's just my opinion, but it's the only one that really matters. They need to rub that stuff off. That's just plain-ole ghetto.

Hello, Cita wants to set the record straight. Just because there's a certain style of clothing out in the stores doesn't mean it's for you. I've seen some sistas walking around with those low-waisted jeans and halter-tops, sporting a belly-button ring. Now, I do admit, that's a very sexy look, and I can pull it off very well. But if you have a huge stomach or have a couple of rolls, or look like you're ready to deliver a baby and you're not pregnant, then you need to be slapped for wearing something like that. If your stomach is not flat, please put those clothes back. 'Nuff said.

$\mathbf{S}$istas who wear weaves, please try and keep it maintained, especially if you are trying to pass it off as your own. I'm going keep it real up in here, I don't care if some of y'all get mad or not. First of all, the tracts of your pieces are not supposed to show like it's a style. Get your lazy butt to the beauty shop and get your weave tightened. Another tip, if you've got two inches of kinky new growth exposed and your weave is bleached blond and straight to your waist, you really need to run, not walk, to the nearest salon. Because your tacky ass is not fooling anybody.

Hold up, can Cita holla at ya? Why is it that in the summertime women with the ugliest feet want to wear the prettiest, most delicate-looking sandals? I hate to see feet with heels that look like dry, ashy potatoes sticking out of a pretty sandal. What's even worse is when each toe is covered with double corns, and bunions are sticking three inches out of the shoe. Ladies, that is not cute at all. Do us all a favor and put those sandals back on the rack and get yourself a pair of sneakers.

If you don't know if you're one of those women with ugly feet, let Cita give you two hints. Hint number one: You seem to notice that every time you go into the Korean nail shop they all start arguing among each other that they don't want to give you a pedicure, and they have to flip a coin to see who gets stuck working on your feet. Hint number two: They have to use garden shears to cut your toe nails and a brick to scrape the dead skin off your bunions that are as big as onions. Then you know you've got some ugly-ass feet.

This message is for the Nubian queens who rock the braided hairstyles. I know that braids are the most convenient hairstyle in the world, but why do so many women forget that they need to get them done again? Nothing is worse than looking at someone's matted-up braids filled with lint that should have been redone nine months ago. The braids are hanging by threads on to the new growth. It looks so bad I just want to sneak up and snatch those braids off their heads. The same ladies who walk around like this are complaining that they can't get a man. Hmm, I wonder why?

Mamacita wants to pass this advice along to the braid wearers. WARNING! WARNING! If you see your hairline creeping further and further back, stop getting those styles that are so tight you can't close your eyes at night. Word, I know this woman whose hairline now starts five inches back from her forehead and she's scraping tufts of hair with Vaseline trying to pass it off as baby hair. That's pathetic.

Cita wants to pose this question: Is there such a thing as wearing too many hairstyles at the same time? I say, hell yeah. Yesterday I was on the avenue and saw this chick walking around with Afro puffs on the side of her head, some braids hanging in her face, paste-on extension curls, and a straight weave ponytail hanging down her back. She was walking down the boulevard twisting her behind like she was da bomb. Now I know black women have versatile hair, but that was ridiculous.

Cita wants to know, is there such a thing as wearing too much weave? I never really thought about that until I was at the electric company paying a bill the other day and went to speak to the customer service rep. I stared at her for a few minutes totally confused. Honestly, I couldn't tell the front of her head from the back. It looked like she shaved off the tails from a whole stable of horses and stuck it on the top of her head.

Some of you women are taking color coordination to a whole 'nother level. Lately I've seen women walking around with bright hair that looks like colors from the Crayola crayon box. Shoot, I believe in looking fashionable but forest green and sky blue hair? Get real. At least wait for the Caribbean Day Parade in Brooklyn, New York, so you'll have the excuse that your hair color matches your costume. But remember, that excuse is only good for one day.

I was at the airport a few weeks ago, and I saw this man checking me out. Who could blame him? I looked good. Anyhoo, the woman who was with him got mad. She gave me a dirty look and had the nerve to call me a hoochie heifer and said my show on BET sucked. I told that playa hater she needed to take off that strawberry blond wig because it didn't match her black, bushy eyebrows and gray mustache and beard. I dissed her so bad, she started screaming and security came rushing over. Cita says, if you can't handle the heat, then don't play with fire. If you step to me, you better come correct.

Don't you just hate the phony perpetrators? You know, the ones who run out and get the latest trendy items to prove they're a baller. They always have the newest cellular phone and pagers that hit the market, and they will have a huge satellite dish sitting on their roof. The dish is so big, you could swear it's almost bigger than the house. And they're always rocking designer gear like Fubu and Sean John, but when you see them in the supermarket, they're wearing dark shades as they pull out a wad of food stamps to pay for their groceries.

Lately, a lot of jiggas have been stepping to yours truly, Ms. Cita, with a mouthful of gold teeth. Sometimes they'll have diamond chips on top of each individual gold tooth. This leads me to think, is putting gold on every tooth in your mouth a clever conversation starter, or a tragic fashion mistake? Well, it's a tragedy when you put all your paychecks for the next year into your mouth. Then when it's time to take me out to dinner you can't afford it. I'm sorry, but a Happy Meal from McDonald's or a Snack Pack from KFC just ain't cutting it for me.

Strange Folks

My Aunt Verna from Alabama wanted to stay with me for two weeks this past summer. When she reached the bus terminal, she called me on the phone and told me she had brought a few cats with her and hoped I wouldn't mind. I was ready to scream. Folks have a lot of nerve bringing a bunch of smelly animals with them to your house.

Anyhoo, I left the key for her under the doormat and told her I'd be home later. When I came home I saw cats all over the place. They were on the couch, on the chair, on top of the television, and on the floor. Aunt Verna even had one wrapped around her neck. But then I noticed something strange—none of the cats were moving. They were all dead and stuffed. Oh, hell no, those stiff cats had to go! Aunt Verna grabbed her chest saying she was going to have a heart attack if I got rid of her cats. I told her not to worry, I had the paramedics on speed dial. That very night Aunt Verna and her trunkful of dead cats were on the Greyhound bus headed back to Alabama. Cita don't allow no mess like that up in her house.

My friend Sheneska called me up one day telling me her grandmother's pet poodle, Fido, just died and they were going to have an elegant memorial service for him. The funeral was going to cost about ten thousand dollars. What is wrong with these folks? Do you know what I could do with that money? Get some slamming outfit and some fierce shoes. That just goes to show you that some people have too much time and money on their hands. They need to go out and get a life, get a man—get something! Ten thousand dollars is just too much damn money to spend on an animal. Shoot, he's dead—he can't appreciate it. Shoot, for ten thousand dollars I can go out and buy a full-length fur in Fido's memory. And somebody please tell those folks from PETA to stop sending me those nasty E-mails.

A few years ago I was in Los Angeles, or La-La Land as I like to call it. My friend Todd, who always tries to out-floss me, invited me to a party up in Beverly Hills. Turns out this party was a wedding for two dogs—a cocker spaniel and a beagle. Personally, I was not amused. I wore Versace for this? Todd had to be hitting the pipe to invite me to this mess. Then, I heard a lot of women at the party were mad: jealous because the damn dogs were getting married and they were still single! I tell you, weddings can bring out the playa hating to a whole new level. Word to the wise, that bouquet toss can be a dangerous part of the wedding. Those single women will stomp you if you don't watch out.

The local zoo sent yours truly, Ms. Cita, a letter asking if I wanted to volunteer. The letter said, "Make your life happy and complete. Mingle with the elephants when you sweep up their compounds. Get a kick out of life when you bathe the giraffes. Learn to love the lions when you water their cages." Let me say this, sistas don't usually go out of their way for this type of volunteering. Life has got to be pretty damn pathetic for me to start embracing the smell of elephant dung. I wrote back telling them I was the queen of content. My time could be better spent shopping or getting my hair did. Don't write to me with no more nonsense unless you're hooking me up with a fine brotha with a pocket full of cheddar, and I'm not talking Velveeta.

Cita gonna take a moment to pause for the cause and drop some knowledge. Remember them good old-school days when kids got mad at each other and said, "I'm gonna kick yo butt at three o'clock," and you would be sweating bullets because Shaquan or Jamal was waiting to beat your behind? If you ran home and told your mama she would give you a choice, either face up to that snotty-nosed kid or go for a round with her and a belt. Those were the good old days, word. But nowadays, kids are taking it to a whole new level. Especially the white kids. If they get mad, they'll take everybody out or try to blow up the school. Picking on the class nerd sure ain't what it used to be. They know how to give new meaning to the phrase *Revenge of the Nerds*.

It was a hot summer day in Manhattan when I saw this fine brotha walking about fifteen dogs. He said Cita, girl let me conversate with you for a minute. I looked at him and said you sure love dogs. He said he was doing it for the money, that he was a professional dog walker. Then he pulled out a bunch of plastic Ziploc bags and started scooping up dog poo from all the dogs who started crapping at exactly the same time, and I have to say the aroma was not pleasant. Picture this, while he's on his knees scooping, he's asking me out on a date. I'm sorry, but that's nasty. He could not have been in his right mind asking for the digits of the fabulous one while scraping dog poo off the sidewalk. I said no way baby. I cannot roll with a man who picks up dog droppings for a living. In the back of my mind, I knew the smell of his job would always cling to him. There's no way I could go out with him. I'm sorry, but Cita does not do sympathy dates, not in this lifetime.

Cheap Folks

Some folks are so damn cheap—they won't even put heat on in the house in the wintertime when it's freezing outside and you can blow smoke rings with your breath indoors. I was seeing this guy who owned a house, but he was so damn cheap he'd rather burn charcoal in a barbecue grill than turn on the heat. Talking about we can kill two birds with one stone—stay warm and have some barbecue ribs. Now ain't this romantic? Ms. Cita got out of there, it's obvious he had inhaled a little too much toxic smoke and had lost all the good sense God gave him.

Ms. Cita is gonna start calling folks out. You know you are a cheap backwoods country ass if you wash all your clothes in the tub. I knew this woman who didn't have a washing machine and who never stepped foot inside a laundromat, saying she'd rather wash all her clothes in the tub. She said all that scrubbing gave her soft hands. Okay, somebody hold me back. When the hell does putting your hands in detergents, bleach, and ammonia give you soft hands? Hell, if you really want to know, her hands were hard and dry, just like a slab of concrete. Truth was, she was just too triflin' and cheap to spend a few quarters to wash and dry.

The ultimate in cheapness is folks who never take a shower or bath because they are afraid to use too much water. Terrified of one day getting a water bill that's a few dollars more than they expected, so they always wash up in the bathroom sink. I'll bet they pray for a heat wave so the kids will open up the street hydrants. Then they'll sneak into the hydrant water with a bar of soap so they can get a real shower. Hmm, now that I think about it, they're not just cheap, they're crazy, too.

My Uncle Clyde has got to be the cheapest man I ever met. The man has a bundle of money but refuses to spend a dime. He volunteered to take my cousin Louisa, who's eighty years old, from New York to Virginia in his car and asked me to come along. Now his car is a Ford Thunderbird that's over thirty years old. He doesn't have a CD or tape player, he just has an eight-track player— and that's broke. Uncle Clyde had the nerve to say we can sing along the way to keep ourselves company. Oh, hell no, I love my family, but I will not subject myself to some off-key, don't-know-the-words, sour-note singing for eight straight hours. Blood is thicker than water, but unnecessary bloodshed is a true tragedy.

Cita's gonna say it again. I can't stand no cheap-ass folks. Especially the kind that will embarrass you at the all-you-can-eat buffet. And, Lawd, don't let shrimp or crab be part of the dinner, cheap-ass folks will lose their minds. My friend Lucreita brought her cousin Jamalia along with us to the Chinese-food buffet and she had the nerve to start stuffing her fake Louis Vuitton pocket-book with seafood. Now ain't nothing worse than get-ting caught stealing food at a buffet. Those waiters gathered around our table and cussed her out in Chinese. I don't know what they said, but I know they told her off. All the other customers were looking at our table, pointing, and laughing. I was so mad I wanted to snatch Jamalia's cheap weave off her head and run out the door.

Cheap and greedy are a stupid combination. I was at this church dinner and they were serving a potluck dinner. Everything was nice until the waiter wanted to clean off the table. This foolish man started hollering, talking about he wanted a doggie bag to take his food home. But he didn't have anything on his plate but a pile of chewed-up chicken bones and gnawed-up neck bones. That fool said, well that's the best part. He could suck the juice out of the bones when he watched television later that night. You know, some folks you just can't take anywhere. They will embarrass you.

Two weeks ago I met this fly brother who said he was an entrepreneur. He claimed he had his own business and could take me to nice places and buy me nice things, keep me iced up. I thought it was my lucky day. I had met me a baller. Then I saw him at the grocery store with all these garbage bags filled with cans and bottles. He explained to me that was his business, going through the streets, looking through garbage cans, collecting cans for money. He had the nerve to tell me I could work for him. Grab a shopping cart and start collecting, he would give me two cents for every can or bottle I found. I started laughing so hard I couldn't speak. Picture that, me, Cita, the epitome of beauty and fabulousness, walking through the streets collecting some cans. Then I turned around and left his cheap, crazy ass standing there. I mean, why should I start screaming on someone who obviously is a few cards short of a full deck?

Before Ms. Cita was a superstar VJ at BET, she used to work at a desk job for a newspaper. We had a cafeteria there, and everybody used to bring lunch and put it in the refrigerator. Then, somebody started stealing lunches out of the fridge. Every day someone's lunch would be missing. When that cheap thief stole mine, that was the last straw. I left both a chocolate cake and a chocolate milkshake containing chocolate-flavored Ex-Lax in the fridge. I knew that crook wouldn't be able to resist that. Then, all I had to do was keep an eye on the bathrooms. By four o'clock that afternoon I had my answer, this chickenhead named Cynthia was stinking up the bathroom. Justice was served.

Nasty
Folks

Cita wants to take a minute and talk about those nasty people. The ones who act like they don't have no sense in their heads when they go to a restaurant. Why is it that when you're about to eat your delicious meal, the fool from the next table, who has finished, decides to pull out a napkin and loudly blow his nose? Excuse you, but didn't your mama teach you any manners? I can't stand those nasty-ass triflin' people. The least you can do is haul your ass up from the table and go to the rest-room so I can enjoy my meal in peace.

I can't stand no nasty people. Cita's going to tell you what really grosses her out. Every winter people get the sniffles and runny noses. Okay, I can understand the change in weather will screw up your sinuses. Just get yourself some Kleenex and clean yourself up. But what irks my last nerve is people who don't have a tissue, and they will squeeze their nose and blow snot out onto the ground. Ughhh, I hate seeing people do that. It's just plain-old nasty and disgusting and you need to stop.

Cita wants to know, what is the fascination that people have with digging up their noses? Word, I have seen some grown folks digging up their noses like there was some kind of prize up there. Then, after they finish digging, they pull out their boogers and examine them and rub them between their fingers. That's just nasty. And I'm not even going to talk about the folks who taste what they find. I don't want to gross myself out.

Why is it that the nastiest people always want to volunteer their cooking services for the office party? I know this woman, Lulu, who has about ten cats and dogs. Now, I'm not saying that everybody who has a house full of animals is nasty, but she is. Lulu lets her cats jump up on the kitchen counter, on the stove, and on the table. There's cat and dog hair everywhere and her house smells like a litter box that hasn't been changed in a year. I make it my business to find out what dish she's making for the party—so I can avoid it.

I can't stand nasty people who always want to dig their hands into my plate of food. Just because we're out after work together, hanging out and enjoying buffalo wings and chicken tenders, doesn't mean I want you to put your nasty hands in my food. There are a lot of folks out there who don't like to wash their hands after they visit the restroom. I know, because I've seen them. I don't know why, but folks always think I'm joking when I say to keep your paws out of my plate. The next time they reach for my food, I think I'll just drive the message home by plunging my fork into their hand. Believe me, they'll start to get the point.

Relatively Speaking

My cousin Tasha is one of those bragging relatives who gets on my nerves in a major way. She'll pull up to my house, driving her Cadillac Escalade, with the speakers blasting to announce her presence. Then she'll step out wearing a Tommy Hilfiger pantsuit and flossing some big ice. And before she get inside my front door, she loves to start bragging, I got this and I got that. Okay, hold up. I ain't hating up in here, but if you have a mouthful of missing teeth you are not coming correct. How are you going to act like you're all that when the last couple of teeth left in your mouth are swinging from the roots? All the other relatives are scared to tell her, but one day I just told her, you need to get your jacked up teeth fixed. Ooh, she got so mad, like it was a surprise to her that she had messed-up teeth. Shoot, sometimes you just have to shut folks down.

I think every family has a cousin who wants to compete with you. My cousin Gayle gets on my last nerve. If a baller puts a nice piece of ice on my finger, that heifer will run to the jewelry store, max out her credit card and put herself in debt to compete with me. Then she'll make up a story that some man just bought her a ring and it becomes a battle of the bling-blings. What makes it so bad is the next week she'll be asking to borrow money from me so she'll have bus fare to go to work. I wish someone would start a therapy group called Playa Haters Anonymous so sick people like her can get the help they so desperately need.

My Aunt Bee always shows up at the family reunion bragging about her five kids. She always has pictures of her five boys posing with their cars. In her eyes, that shows how successful they are. She'll say, "This is Terrence and he's driving a BMW, and my baby boy, Cinque, is struggling so he's driving a Honda Civic." Aunt Bee never mentions what kind of job they have or how they're doing, just what kind of car they drive. I'll ask her questions about them, and she'll start telling me what expensive features they have on their cars like how much they paid for the rims. Personally, she makes me crazy and I'm glad family reunions are only every couple of years.

Family reunions are always a funny experience. Sometimes you'll have those relatives who spring out the woodwork that you haven't heard from in years. My relatives who live in West Virginia are real ghetto. They pulled up to the picnic area in this old car that was basically held together by duct tape. That tape was everywhere, on the windshield, on the doors, on the rearview and side mirrors, on the seats. Then they pulled a cooler full of chitterlings off the hood of the car. When they opened the lid and the scent of those funky pig parts hit me, I knew it was time to go.

One time I went to a family picnic with this new man I was dating. The mama of his baby was there, and she brought her other two kids along. Boy, those were some bad-ass kids, and when they got together with their cousins from the projects, they were even worse. One little girl in particular, Takeysha, got on my nerves. First of all, I don't like to talk about people's kids, but she looked like a little troll. She was about five, had a smart mouth, and ran around squirting people in the face with a water gun. The last straw was when she wet my hair. Oh no, you don't ruin the diva's hairdo. I grabbed that water gun from her and hit her with a burst of water that knocked her back about five feet. There is no shame in my game. Cita will take you out. I don't care if you haven't reached puberty yet.

Every year at the family barbecue, my Uncle Louie insists on working the grill after he's drank more than twelve cans of malt liquor. A big argument always breaks out because he's drunk and nobody wants him on the grill. Then Uncle Louie always go through the same routine. He grabs a can of lighter fluid and some matches and claims he will light himself up if we don't let him help out. It's crazy because he always ends up burning all the hot dogs, chicken, and ribs. I swear, one year I'm going to dare him to light himself up. And when the paramedics come to get him, at least I can enjoy some barbecue that's not all burnt up.

Now Cita knows that she's not the only one who has those so-called Christian cousins that visit every summer. I dread when my cousins from Texas come to town. All they want to know is where the party is. They will hit every bar and club, drink liquor until they're staggering, and if anyone gives them a funny look, they're ready to start fighting. I am so embarrassed because the New York City Police Department has my home phone number posted on the bulletin board. They are constantly calling for me to come and pick up my relatives from the precinct. But, on Sunday morning, my cousins will be the first ones sitting in the church pews ready to shout Hallelujah and drop to their knees speaking in tongues.

Celebrity Show-and-Tell

Toni Braxton

Okay, I love Toni and have supported her since her first album. But after her career blew up, she started going through some changes, wanted to spice up her image to be some kind of sex goddess. She went and got some cosmetic enhancements, y'all know what I'm talking about, went from flat to busty within twenty-four hours. Then she decided to get some publicity for herself by posing butt naked on the cover of *Vibe* magazine. This was supposed to shock everybody 'cause her daddy was a preacher and she grew up a holy roller. Pleeeease, that didn't shock Cita, I always said it's them quiet ones you got to watch out for.

Now I love to shop for some fly clothes, but Toni would have me all out in every boutique on Rodeo Drive in Beverly Hills maxing out credit cards. The sales clerk would tell her that she was over her limit, but Toni would start screaming she could afford the clothes and didn't they know who she was? That was the first hint her ass was in trouble. Then Toni would call Ms. Cita up all the time begging for me to lend her some duckets to get her weave tightened. I tried to tell her to stop buying all that fake hair from the Koreans, it was going to bankrupt her, but she wouldn't listen. Well, now she got a new husband and hopefully her money situation is tight and she'll stop blowing up my phone 'cause Cita's tired of being known as Cita bank.

Eminem

Yo, Eminem, that single, "The Real Slim Shady," was hot. Yeah, when your album dropped it was da bomb, it blew up all over the place. Em crossed the color line, showed that white guys can hang in the rap game. Big up to Dr. Dre, the producer, for originality, personality, and some slamming dope beats. Eminem won a Grammy, got major publicity and recognition, and got into some trouble with the law. Could somebody holla at Cita and let me know why Emmy is still so angry? His album sold millions of copies, he's no longer living in a trailer park eating government cheese. Shouldn't his ass be smiling and happy? He is one angry blond. I know lots of rappers built a successful career on pretending they had to attend anger-management classes. Much respect to Ice Cube, Ice-T, and Dr. Dre, to name a few. But somebody needs to pull Emmy's collar and tell him he needs to chill. The thug appeal is only good for so long. I hear Will Smith is about to drop a new album, which means happy, feel-good music is back to stay. Y'all gansta rappers hear that? Time to change your tune. Start smiling, put some pop beats in your records and chase that check.

Joan and Melissa Rivers

Oh, my gawwwd, it's the demonic duo! This mother-daughter tag team can do some serious playa hating on the red carpet at the award shows. One year I came to the Grammy Awards and they dissed me. Can you believe it? They had something to say about yours truly, sexy Mamacita. I was wearing a bright red leather pantsuit and I had my hair colored red to match the outfit. Well, those witches had the nerve to say my butt was too big for the pants. Joan said she thought somebody called the fire department, because from behind I looked like a large, red fire truck. And that witch also said my hair looked like the red flames of hell and she wished someone would grab the extinguisher and put it out.

Joan Rivers, with her reconstructed face, needs to sit

her ass down. Doesn't she know all those hot lights at the awards show can melt all those surgically enhanced parts? And her daughter, Melissa, is no prize either with her toothpick shape. Y'all both need to go get a burger and fries and gain some weight. You are both envious of me because I am curvy and fine. That's right, I'm telling you playa haters like it is, and I just shut you both down. So from now on when you see Ms. Cita on the red carpet, you can just talk to the hand.

Jennifer Lopez

Now me and Jennifer go way back. I have known her since the days of riding the number-six train to the Bronx. Way back in the days when she looked like every other Puerto Rican girl on the block with black, curly hair—now she be blond claiming she ain't close friends with Miss Clairol. Girl, stop lying, I see the peroxide bottle in your pocketbook. Okay, let's not get it twisted, I ain't hating on J.Lo. It's all good, go and chase that check—fatten yo pockets with the cheddar. It's a little known fact, but me and J.Lo were the last two finalists going up for the spot as a fly-girl dancer on *In Living Color*. Let's keep it real, I had that role in my back pocket. I was blowing up the spot with my fresh hip-hop moves. All of a sudden, I found myself facedown on the floor. Now J.Lo will say I fell off the stage, but Cita ain't crazy, I know I was pushed. Anyhoo, Keenan Ivory Wayans offered me the part, after he broke up the fight between me and Miss Lopez. But because my ankle was broken, I had to pass on the part. So, J.Lo became a fly girl, which was the start of her career, and the rest is history thanks to the fabulous one, *moi*.

Christina Aguilera

"What a girl wants . . ." Yeah, that was a nice jam, but what Christina really needs to do is eat a few more meals—she's too skinny, looks like she's starving for a Supersize order of Mickey D's hamburger and fries. Too many of these little starlets fall into that trap of believing the smaller their dress size, the hotter their career will get. Shoot, there's so many women in denial of their feminine fat and womanly curves that they are now a size zero. Christina, you're going to need more than a genie in a bottle when it's time to cash yo check and the teller at the check-cashing place can't even see your narrow ass. I saw little Ms. Aggie at one of the awards shows where she was rocking long, blond cornrows and a little skimpy outfit. She could hardly get out of the chair. Them synthetic braids were so heavy—they weighed more than her. Girl, you better listen to Cita and stay yo skinny behind out of those African hair-braid shops—at least until you gain a few pounds.

Monica Lewinsky

Ms. Cita can't stand that money-hungry fat hussy by the name of Monica Lewinsky. Now before y'all start blowing up my phone defending her with excuses like, she was in love with the president and her intentions was good, let me make my point. That woman was a supreme hoochie and a calculating hussy with dollar bills in her eyes who went after the leader of the free world. Okay, I'll give her props for aiming high and going after the biggest baller, the prez, but that's it. Any woman who keeps a dirty, stained dress sitting in the closet, and has no intentions of cleaning it, is twisted. Believe Cita, that dress was collateral—her ticket to the big time. When she got a book deal to spill her guts, I was mad as hell. But I really went through the roof when Weight Watchers offered her a phat contract to lose weight. Shoot, nobody ever offered Cita a lousy green one dollar bill to drop a pound. How come that heifer was getting paid? I calmed down when I came up with a plan to insure Ms. Lewinsky would not collect those bonus checks. How could she resist those chocolate cakes, pies, and cookies I kept shipping anonymously to her house? Now, if I ever see her on the street, I'll tell her she can just walk her chubby ass to the unemployment office and get a good ole nine-to-five like everybody else.

Britney Spears

Yours truly, Ms. Cita, wants to talk about that little blond bimbo by the name of Britney Spears. You know, the chick who recycles Janet Jackson's old dance moves and tries to pass them off as her original stuff. I ain't playa hating because she sold millions of copies of her albums, I'm just keeping it real, exposing the truth. Let me tell y'all when she came out with that song, "Oops! . . . I Did It Again," there's a line in it where Britney says, "I'm not innocent." Damn right, yo ass ain't innocent. After we saw her break out almost naked and striptease at the MTV Video Music Awards show. Then she had the nerve to show up at the Super Bowl with her boobs busting out her top. Damn, her mama lets her walk out the house like that? I guess Britney and her mom figure that it's all about the Benjamins. The real innocent party in all this scandal is Justin Timberlake, that kid from *NSync who's dating her. Ain't it a shame when a nice guy has no idea that the girl he's dating is one of the biggest hoochies out there? I know his boys be trying to tell him to watch out, but he is truly a clueless wonder. You know Britney is just using him for her image. Shoot, Cita knows what time it is.

Lil' Kim

Lil' Kim and Ms. Cita used to be real tight. Hanging out in Brooklyn, rockin' the mike at block parties, shopping for gear at the mall. We would make all the jiggas head turn at the clubs, they would step to us and beg to buy us drinks. But once the little one got a record deal, she changed. She went and bought some discount boobs, got some rainbow-colored wigs, fake eyes, and she started buying clothes four sizes too small. Word, I think she started shopping in the children's section the way some of them outfits looked on her.

Cita just gonna preach the truth and keep it real.

Mary J. Blige

Everybody just loves Mary J. Blige. People be like, "Mary, Mary, that's my girl, I love her." Cita's gonna give it to you straight—Mary's mean as hell. Don't get it twisted, I've known Mary since she was living in the hood, at the Yonkers projects. We would hang out at the nail shop in the mall and get our nails done. One day these hoochies came up in there, trying to jump the line, and had the nerve to ask if they could pay with food stamps. Mary started riffin', telling them they better go home to their three and four kids before she gave them a beatdown. Personally, I did not want to fight because I just got my four-inch acrylic tips airbrushed and studded with rhinestones, but if I had to back my girl up, I would have. Just recently, Mary started calming down. But a couple of months ago we had an argument and ain't speaking because she said Lil' Kim keeps it real and represents. I had to scream on her because Kim is as fake as a three-dollar bill. Now Kim is her new best friend. Check out their MAC Cosmetics ad. Big question: Why is Lil' Kim sitting with her legs wide open, looking like she's trying to sell more than make-up? So, right now, I'm just waiting for Mary to hit me on my two-way pager, cell phone, beeper, or E-mail with an apology.

Ice-T

Ice-T is one of the original old-school gangstas. He started off his career as a rapper and had everybody in law enforcement mad at one of his rap songs. Word, he was public enemy number one on the most wanted list. But mad props to Ice-T, he knows how to flip the script. Homeboy held it down in the movie *New Jack City*—and had the nerve to play the role of a cop! He's a hot commodity in Hollywood now. Any television show that needs a in-yo-face kinda Negro will call on Ice-T. I swear all he has to do is growl at the casting director and scare them into giving him a part. He knows how to cut his eyes like a machete—being mean has paid off for him. I heard he's got a fly crib in Callie. Ice-T's definitely got a pocket full of cheddar.

Pamela Anderson

Pamela is a chick straight from the trailer park who got over big-time in Hollywood. No talent—she can't act—her real talent is walking around town with her boobs on display. Doesn't she remind you of somebody who should be in a cartoon running from the Tasmanian Devil or Wile E. Coyote? Remember last year when she had those enomorous fake boobs and then got them reduced, saying that what you see now is real? Somebody hold me down. Who does she think she's fooling? I swear, if I see her in Beverly Hills, Cita is gonna run up on her and scream, *"Fake!"*

Letters to Cita

Dear Cita,

I'm thirty years old, but I'm dating this guy who's twenty-five. He is really good looking, and he works as a DJ at a night club. My problem is all these hoochies keep throwing themselves at my man. I could be standing right there and they'll flirt with him right in front of me. Please tell me what to do.

Signed,

Frustrated and Upset

Dear Frustrated and Upset,

Cita can see what your problem is. You need to grow a backbone and keep those hoochie heifers away from your man. There ain't no way a woman is going to flirt with my man while I'm standing there. Word of advice, the next time a woman starts talking to your boo, wrap your pocketbook strap around your hand and start swinging your pocketbook real hard. Those women will think you're about to jump violent and leave in a hurry. Good luck.

Dear Cita,

I'm fourteen years old and I love you. I think you are so fly and you're always rockin' some fresh gear. This is my problem, I'm dating this guy who wants to be a rapper. He's really good and sounds just like Ja Rule. He wants to have a son so we can dress him up in gold chains and Baby Gap and Phat Farm. I believe he's talented and that he's going to make it, plus he told me that he loves me. Should I go ahead and have the baby?

Signed,

Happy but Confused

Dear Happy but Confused,

Thanks for the compliments. You sound like a real sweet girl. My advice to you is to finish your education before you even think about having a baby. If he loves you, he will wait. Besides, it could be true that he's a talented rapper, but he should also finish school and get a recording deal before you get married and take that walk down the aisle.

Good luck to ya.

Dear Cita,

I've been dying to write this letter and tell you off. Who do you think you are? You are always putting people down, snapping on them like you've got it going on. Meanwhile, you are so ghetto that you need to be the one to sit down. You think you are so sexy, but I don't think you are. I know you had a boob job so you need to stop dissing people.

Signed,

Tameka

Dear Tameka,

It sounds like you have a lot of pent-up anger inside of you. I know who I am, do you have a clear definition of who you are? Listen, baby, don't hate the player, hate the game. Cita never said she was against cosmetic enhancement, I'm all for self-improvement. You seem to be very upset that I'm shining so brightly. My advice to you is find out what makes you happy and go for it. That way when you tune in *Cita's World* you won't be so mad watching me blow up the spot.

Dear Cita,

You are so fly. I think you are the hottest VJ out there. My friends and I love you and wanted to ask your opinion about something. If an artist had one big hit and disappears off the charts, don't you think record companies should try and bring them back? You know, revive their careers? It's a shame, but a lot of singers who used to have careers are now working in the fast-food restaurants.

Signed

Janet K.

Dear Ms. K.,

It's so nice of you to drop Cita a letter. I'm glad you feel that the record companies should listen to my authority because I believe my opinion is the only one that really matters. I strongly feel that the one-hit wonders should stay asleep in music heaven. They've had their fifteen minutes of fame. If you can't hang, you will get kicked to the curb. It's the way of the world.

Peace.

Dear Cita,

I wanted to write you for advice about this guy I'm seeing. His name is Ricky and he has a baby by this girl named Tomi. He's still seeing her, but he wants to break up with her. I really like him 'cause he's really cute and buys me nice things. The only thing is Tomi is one of my good friends, so I feel kinda bad. What should I do?

Signed,

Desperate in Chicago

Dear Desperate in Chicago,

Girlfriend, you know you are wrong for trying to take Ricky away from Tomi. It sounds to me that he's running a game on her and he's going to do the same on you. Besides, if Tomi's your friend, you should step off and find somebody else. And by the way, all those nice things he's buying for you should probably be going toward the baby. Cita says find yourself another boo and save yourself a lot of heartache.

Strictly My Opinion

145

Artists That Get Mad Props

Nas—Oww, Nas is aiiright. Cita likes your style, boo-boo.

Lil' Bow Wow—He's just too cute. His mama had better keep a real close eye on him before one of the girls from 3LW snatch him up.

Case—His song "I'm Missing You" was off da hook.

Missy Elliott—Mad props to my girl Missy. She is a woman who is definitely on top of her game in the music business.

Timbaland—He keeps hitting us off with those dope beats. Forget the haters, Tim, keep doing yo thing.

Barry White—After all these years, Barry's voice still rules. That man has got one sexy voice.

Nate Dogg—When he puts his vocals on the track, the song just blows up. Everybody better recognize.

Eve—Her album *Scorpion* is da bomb. And ever since she called me for some fashion tips, her clothes have been looking fresh.

Chris Rock—Chris keeps it real. He doesn't care whose feelings get hurt.

The Rock—He rules the WWF. That's my boo.

Aaliyah—Mad props to Aaliyah. She had a nice singing style, and her acting career was about to explode. She'll always have a special place in our hearts.

Queen Latifah—My girl is on top of her game. She can rap, act, and she had her own talk show. Much respect to the Queen.

Samuel L. Jackson—What can I say? He is just too cool. Sam, when my schedule finally slows down, I am going to co-star in a movie with you. But, I don't know if Hollywood is ready for a movie with the both of us.

OutKast—Those Hotlanta brothas are fierce. They got everybody on notice with that last album they dropped. Love y'all.

Artists Who Need to Sit Down

Sisqo—I'm so glad he took that silver hair dye out of his head. And will somebody give him a new song to sing besides that damn thong song!

Changing Faces—They need to change their act. Those two chicks are getting real tired. I noticed that they are desperately trying to get some attention by wearing hoochie clothes. Only problem, nobody still want to pay them any attention.

New Edition Comeback—No way. That group is played out.

Diana Ross—Okay, it's time to pass the diva crown to somebody else.

Foxy Brown—This little woman tries so hard to be sexy. Baby, if you don't have that natural sex appeal like Cita, you need to give it up.

Macy Gray—Girlfriend, you are a fashion disaster. I caught a performance you gave at an award show. It looked like you went shopping in the dark.

Ray J (Brandy's *Brother*)—I have seen your video and you need to stop fronting. That sexy image is not working.

You need to go back to singing "It's a Small Small World" at Disneyland.

Miss Cleo—the fortune teller—This sista definitely needs to sit down. I called her hotline and asked her if Gary, my last boyfriend, was cheating on me. She said no. Well heifer, how come all those women were blowing up my phone talking all that ying-yang that they're pregnant with his baby?

About the Authors

Glenda Howard is currently the senior editor for the BET Books imprints Sepia and New Spirit. She formerly worked as an editor for St. Martin's Press. A native New Yorker, she currently resides in Queens, NY, with her husband Evan.

Cita made her VJ television debut in 2000 on BET's *Jam Zone* television show. The show was renamed *Cita's World* due to the popularity and broad appeal of its host. The former Washington, DC, resident now lives in Harlem, NY, and describes herself as outgoing, vivacious, talented, gorgeous, and brutally honest. Cita is still single and optimistically looking for Mr. Right.